Leaping Larry's Scary Adventure

A heart-thumping book written by

Dr. Gary

Illustrated by

Chris Sharp

Dr. Gary Books, Chapin, South Carolina

Copyright 2015 by D. Gary Benfield

Illustrations copyright 2015 by D. Gary Benfield, M.D.

All rights reserved. Published in the United States.

ISBN: 978-0-9904942-5-6

The sun was almost down,
but Leaping Larry didn't care. He was having too
much fun showing off for his bug friends,
jumping here and hopping there.

But when he jumped a little too high and hopped a
little too far, he landed...

kirsploosh!...

in the McDoogles' swimming pool.

At first, Larry
wasn't afraid.
After all, frogs are
good swimmers, and the
water felt nice and warm.

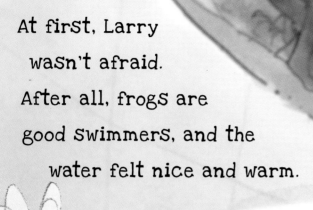

Besides, he knew where he was.
Cindy McDoogle was Larry's best friend.

So, he swam around, looking for a way out of the pool. But each
time he tried to climb out, he slid back in the water. You see,
the sides of the pool were very slippery.

"If only Cindy were here," he sighed. "She would know what to do."

"Ribbit, ribbit!" he called.

But no one answered.

"I am not giving up!" Larry said to himself. "If I just stay calm and save my strength, someone will come along and help me."

After a while, a large leaf floated
down from a nearby tree and
landed on the water.

Grateful to have something to hold on to,
Larry swam over and rested
his head on the leaf.
"Thank you," he whispered.

"You're welcome, Larry," the leaf
replied. "I'm glad to finally meet
you. I'm Mr. Leaf."

"Wow!" a surprised Larry shouted.
"I didn't know leaves could talk!
I guess I'll have to listen more
closely. Nice to meet you
too, Mr. Leaf."

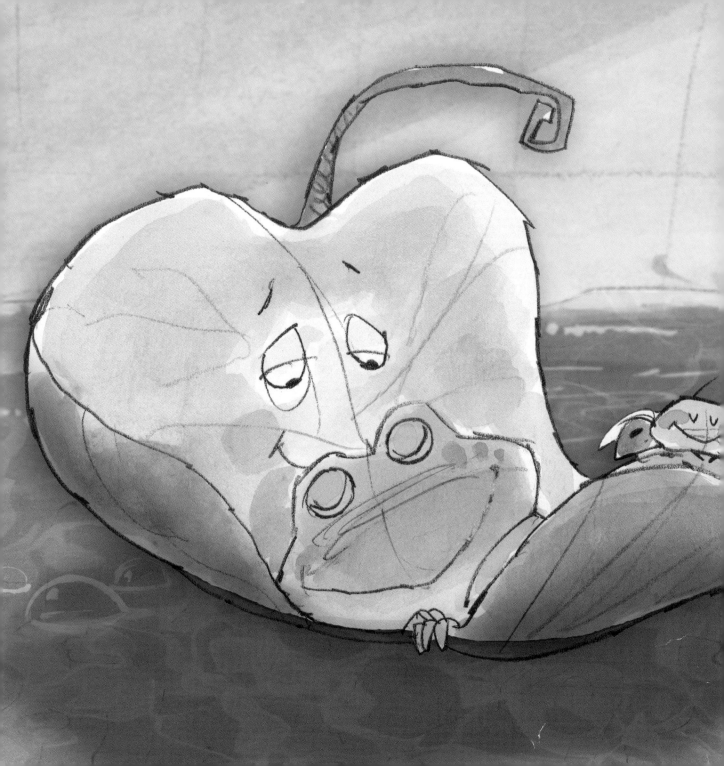

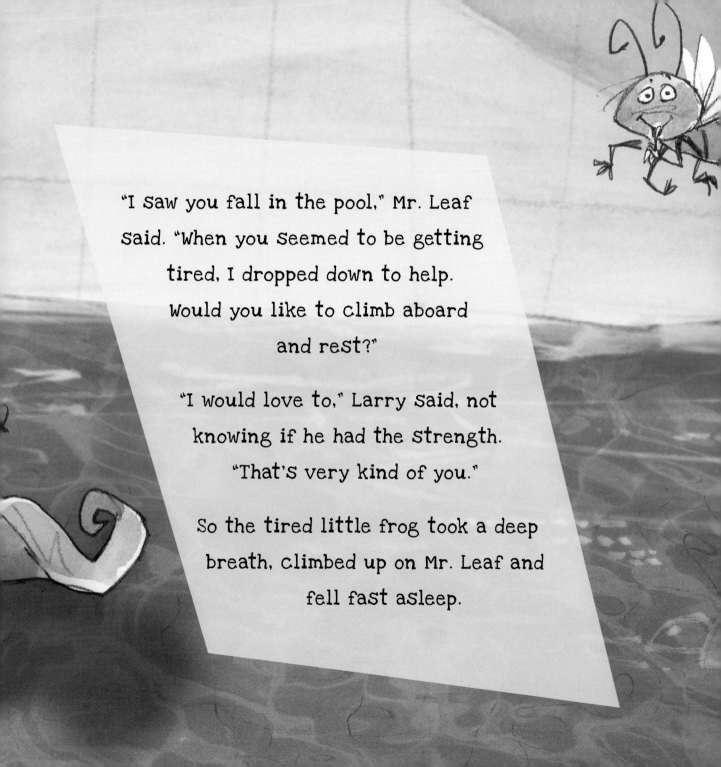

"I saw you fall in the pool," Mr. Leaf said. "When you seemed to be getting tired, I dropped down to help. Would you like to climb aboard and rest?"

"I would love to," Larry said, not knowing if he had the strength. "That's very kind of you."

So the tired little frog took a deep breath, climbed up on Mr. Leaf and fell fast asleep.

As he slept, Larry had a dream. His mom was reading a story to his sisters while his father and brothers were out searching for him.

Sadly, they returned home without him.

Discouraged, but still hopeful, Larry's family joined hands and bowed their heads. Then Larry's father said a prayer, asking for Larry's safe return.

"Hoo! Hoo! WaHoo!" The call of
a hoot owl startled the little
frog and woke him up.

Under a full moon, Larry
spotted the owl.

Afraid the scary creature might see him, Larry slipped quietly into the water.

"Push me over to the shadows," whispered Mr. Leaf. "She may not see us over there."

So, as quietly as he could, Larry pushed Mr. Leaf toward the dark end of the pool.

"That's Momma Owl," whispered Mr. Leaf when they finally reached the shadows. "I've been watching her for several weeks. She's got two babies in a nest up there. She hoots like that when she's about to go hunting for food."

"Food, like little frogs?" Larry whispered, in a panic!

"She usually catches bigger prey and flies them back to the nest," Mr. Leaf replied.

"If you slide under me and tread water, maybe she will think I'm just a floating leaf."

"Then she won't bother us?" Larry asked.

"I hope not," Mr. Leaf replied.

Larry slid underneath Mr. Leaf, just in time.

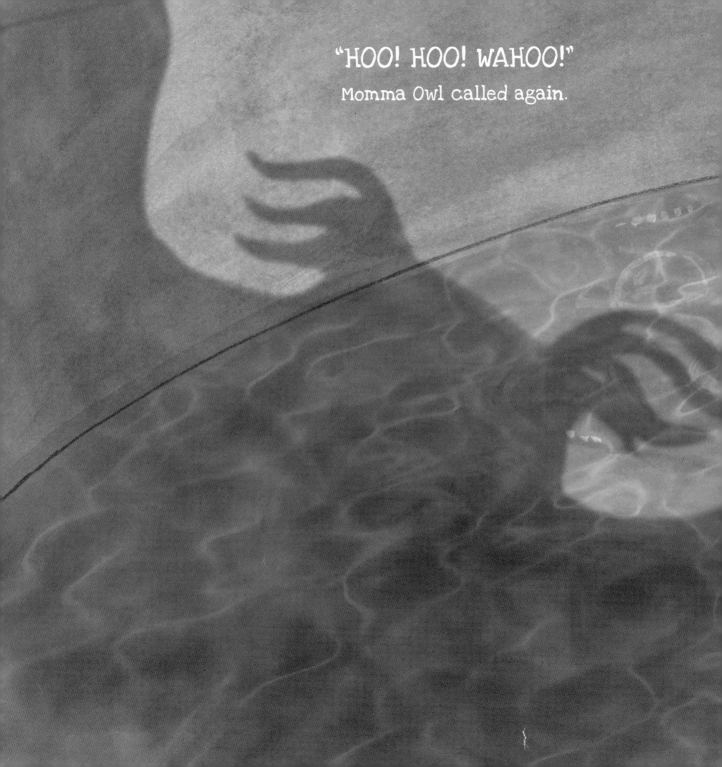

"HOO! HOO! WAHOO!"
Momma Owl called again.

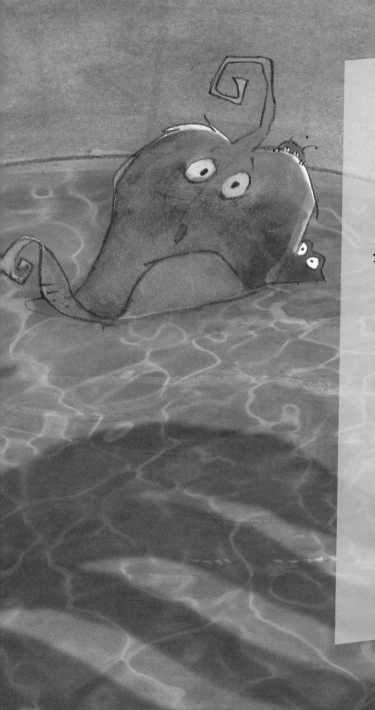

As she circled the pool, the powerful bird soared lower and lower, getting closer and closer. Then she dove for the floating target, her claws open and her sharp beak pointed at Mr. Leaf.

"Stop, Momma Owl!" Mr. Leaf shouted. "Please stop!"

Startled by Mr. Leaf's cry, Momma Owl just missed him and landed by the pool.

"I didn't know it was you, Mr. Leaf," Momma Owl explained. "I'm sure glad you yelled."

"Me too," Mr. Leaf smiled. "Besides, your hungry babies would not find me very tasty."

"That's probably true," Momma Owl laughed. "Speaking of hungry babies," she sighed, "I hear them calling." And off she flew.

"Whew! That was close," Leaping Larry sighed, as he swam out from under Mr. Leaf. "Thank you, thank you."

Relieved, but still tired, Larry climbed back up on Mr. Leaf. For now, at least, he felt safe. Then he fell asleep, not knowing what morning would bring.

"Larry! Larry! Wake up!"
Cindy McDoogle shouted
from the side of the pool as
the sun was coming up.

"I'm sure glad to see you!"
Larry shouted as he
rubbed his eyes.

"What happened?" She called
to her friend.
"Did you fall in?"

"It's a long story," Larry replied. " Can you scoop us up
in your net?"

"Sure thing," she replied. And before they knew it, Larry and
Mr. Leaf were safely on the ground.

Larry was so excited, he did a somersault and landed at Cindy's feet. "Cindy McDoogle," he smiled, "I'd like you to meet my hero, Mr. Leaf. He not only saved me from drowning, but he saved me from Momma Owl."

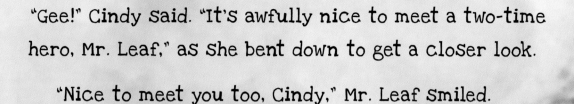

"Gee!" Cindy said. "It's awfully nice to meet a two-time hero, Mr. Leaf," as she bent down to get a closer look.

"Nice to meet you too, Cindy," Mr. Leaf smiled.

"I am going to carry you home," Cindy said to Larry. "You must be tired."

"That's a fine idea," Larry replied. "But I owe my life to Mr. Leaf. He's coming home with me."

Cindy arrived at Larry's house with Larry and Mr. Leaf fast asleep in her arms. Larry's parents were overjoyed to see that their prayers had been answered. But they let Larry and his new friend sleep.

"We'll celebrate later," Larry's father said.

As Cindy got ready to leave, Larry's father handed her a tiny rosebud. "This rose stands for love," he said, "the kind of love I feel for my own children. You are always welcome to visit our humble home."

On that happy note, Cindy headed for home. As she skipped along,
Dexter Duck, a fun-loving friend from her parents' pond,
circled overhead, playfully soaring and diving.

Suddenly, the little girl took off running. "I'll race you to our pool
for a swim," Cindy yelled to Dexter.

"Hey, that's not fair!" the surprised duck yelled as he flew after her.

Yes, things were back to normal, at least for now.

The End

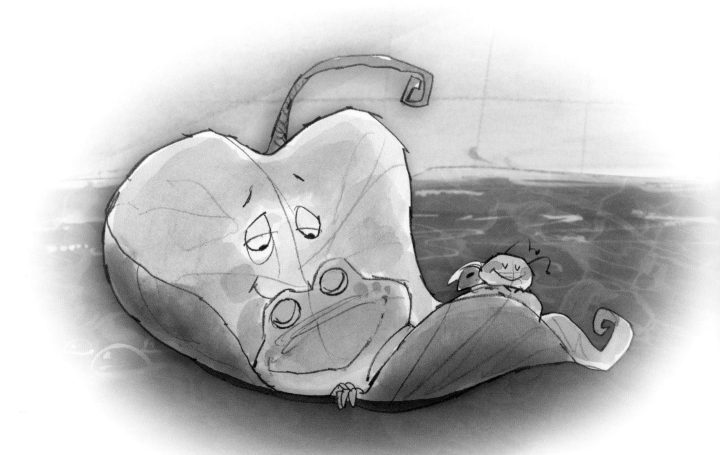

Dedicated to Terree, Laura and Cindy,

three incredible daughters.

No father could be more proud than I.

I would also like to thank Donna Duchek

for helping Leaping Larry and his friends

come alive on the printed page.

D.G.B.